Roland Humphrey is Wearing a WHAT?

Written by Eileen Kiernan-Johnson

Huntley Rahara Press
1960 Stony Hill Road
Boulder, Colorado 80305
To purchase copies of this book, please visit:
RolandHumphrey.com or HuntleyRaharaPress.com

The publisher is not responsible for
websites (or their content) that are not owned by the publisher.

First Edition
ISBN 978-0-615-66655-6

The Illustrations for this book were designed by Katrina Revenaugh.

For Ronan and Kelsey, my brave and beautiful somethingburgers.

"Roland Humphrey, what ARE you wearing?,"
gasped two flummoxed girls, bulging eyes staring.

Ella and Lucy walked up to their friend, examined his outfit and asked him then,
"Is that the color pink we see, there in the stripes across your tee?"

"Oh Roland," sighed Ella, "don't you know? Pink is a color for girls, so
if you don't want people to laugh at you the best color for you to wear is blue.
Also gray and brown, green and tan. Those are the colors for a little man."

"That's right," chimed in Lucy, who readily agreed,
"Here are some helpful pointers you need:

Since you're a boy, pink isn't allowed—
not if you want to be in with the crowd.

For you to fit in, you must eschew
lilac and magenta; opt instead for sky blue."

Roland Humphrey appeared confused
and looked with shame down at his violet-striped shoes.

He'd had no idea about the color rule
explained to him today by his friends at school.

Roland's parents had always said, "It's up to you to choose indigo or red.
Brown or coral, lilac or yellow; which colors you like is up to YOU, young fellow.

And your favorite color can always change. Today it might be aqua, tomorrow bright orange."
But now Roland Humphrey wasn't quite sure if his parents or classmates really knew more.

Nervously preparing for the next day at school,
Roland assembled an ensemble he hoped they'd deem cool.

On bottom he donned a pair of blue jeans
and his long-sleeved shirt was a manly dark green.

Across the shirt's front, however, there flittered
a shiny butterfly adorned with bright glitter.

And to prevent his bangs from obscuring his view,
Roland tucked in his hair a barrette of light blue.

Ella and Lucy first saw him in the school's parking lot.
Together they shrieked, "Roland Humphrey is wearing a WHAT?"

All of the other children spun around to watch,
wondering which rule of apparel today he had botched.

"What's wrong?" a trembling Roland Humphrey queried,
examining his garb through eyes growing teary.

The girls glared at Roland with unmasked disdain.
Correcting this boy was becoming a pain.

Said Lucy: "Roland Humphrey, you are just hopeless.
For boys no adornment—for boys more is less!"

4 Roland Humphrey
what boys
SHOULD like . . .

Ella continued: "Boys can like spaceships that sail through the stars.
They're allowed to wear shirts with trains or with cars.

It's okay for boys to like ball sports played by a team—
football, baseball, or basketball, I mean.

But the things, Roland Humphrey, that you seem to favor
have a decidedly feminine, rather girlish flavor.

Your sparkles are really starting to annoy.
When you wear clothes for girls, how do we know you're a boy?"

Roland listened to the words they had said.
With a heavy heart and hurt feelings, he now hung his head.

Asked Roland: "Is there no exception to this rule?
Why can't I wear whatever I want to school?"

The girls just laughed and rolled their eyes.
Lucy offered in a tone that was dry,

"Tomorrow, Roland Humphrey can you give it a try?
Just for one day, dress like a regular guy?"

Roland Humphrey heaved a deep sigh,
slumped his small shoulders and started to cry.

When Roland Humphrey came home later that day,
his tear-stained cheeks gave his sorrow away.

"What happened, my dear?" asked Mommy with care,
"I'm so sorry you're sad—do you want to share?"

"Well," Roland began in a voice that was small,
"I'm confused by the color rules that limit us all.

I choose things I like, try to be my best me,
not anyone else, just Roland Humphrey.

But the kids tell me it isn't okay
for me to decide for myself if I prefer purple to gray.

The girls at my school dress in all sorts of hues,
but for boys there's so much less we can choose.

For me hockey is fun, but also ballet;
girls can like both—why for boys just one way?

Girls can sport jerseys, pants of dirt brown,
but a boy who wears ruffles is greeted with frowns.

If girls can wear boy clothes, why not the reverse?
Do colors have meaning? Is purple inherently perverse?

If girls can like blue, why can't boys like pink?
These unwritten rules—they're crazy I think!

Mommy, oh mommy, I don't understand
why girls can choose anything but boys simply can't."

Roland Humphrey and his mommy talked it all through—
exploring his feelings, discussing what he might do.

Roland Humphrey mulled it over all night.
Did he show his true colors, or hide them from sight?

The next day he would dress for school with great care,
having thoughtfully weighed how much of his real self to bare . . . .

"Hi friends!" in a bright voice Roland declared.
"You need to know that I'm no longer scared.

Not scared about how you'll view what I'm wearing,
because I've decided that I *need* to be daring.

What matters to me is whether you're kind.
The friends I deserve truly won't mind

if I choose sparkly nailpolish, skirts or clogs,
they'll like me for me, not for my togs.

I'm so much more than what colors or clothes I choose.
And if you judge me on just that, I've got some sad news:

You're the one who misses out.
It's what's inside that really counts.

I'm silly, athletic, creative and smart . . .
and other things too—that's just a start.

So if based on my clothing for me you feel loathing,
then too bad for you because I choose to be the me that is true.

Snazzy, pizazzy—that's the true me . . .
the one and the only Roland Humphrey."

Ella and Lucy came right up to him.
They hugged Roland Humphrey and said with a grin,

"We've thought it all over; we're sorry—we were wrong.
What's the harm in boys wearing princess gowns or sarongs?

It's cool that you're confident in who you are,
that you choose to follow your own north star.

To lose you over pink would be such a waste.
Besides, you have really fabulous taste!

We like you for you, whatever you wear.
You're brave and you're funny. You're senstive and rare.

So, let's be true friends starting today.
Off to the swingset . . . come on, let's go play!"

About the Author:

Eileen Kiernan-Johnson lives in Boulder, Colorado with her husband and two children. This is her first book.